CAFFEINATED PAGES

AF450948

BookSquirrel Publications

CAFFEINATED PAGES

BookSquirrel Publication

Mahadev Totala Nager, Indore (M.P),452001

Regd Under MSME

Website:

www.booksquirrelpublication.com

© **Copyright, 2020, Aashna Chawla**

All rights reserved. No part of this book may be reproduced, stored in a retrieval system, or transmitted, in any form by any means, electronic, mechanical, magnetic, optical, chemical, manual, photocopying, recording or otherwise, without the prior written consent of its writer.

"Caffeinated Pages"

By: Aashna Chawla

ISBN:

English Anthology 1st Edition

Book Formatting:Rubal Choudhary

Cover Design: Ronak Chavda

The opinions/ contents expressed in this book are solely of the author and do not represent the opinions/ standings/ thoughts of BookSquirrel

<u>DISCLAIMER</u>

This Anthology Is A Work Of Fiction.

Our Editors Have Tried Their Best, to Edit The Write Ups And Check The Plagiarism.

All Stories In This Book, Are Unique Work Of Our Writers

ACKNOWLEDGEMENT

This Anthology Would Have Not Been Possible Without The Hard Work Of Our Team And Writers.

The Team Have Put Their Heart And Best To Make This Book

A Success. A Huge Thanks To Every Member Of This Team

And Writers To Give Their Attention And Time To This Project.

This Anthology Is Compiled By Miss. Aashna Chawla.

Thank You Authors For Showing Trust In Us.

And Contributing Your Beautiful Stories With Us.

And Making This Dream Come True, Without You

All This Would Have Stayed A Dream.

Speacial Thanks To Book Squirrel Publications,

For Fulfilling Our Dreams.

Thank You All For Blessings, Wishes And Prayers.

COMPILER

Aashna Chawla, daughter of Mrs. Divya Chawla and Mr. Rajoo Chawla.

A girl who loves to write because the only way she knows to communicate her feelings is by words. She is from Nagpur, Maharashtra.

She is a writer and journalist by profession, she is currently studying Bachelors in Arts in English Literature.

She started writing two years ago. As in the very begining she always underestimated her emotions until, she got that her emotions are the only way she can write in.

She started posting on her instagram and received appreciation and that motivated her. And she finally established her instagram page named,

UNVOICED HEART.

The title says many things itself. Maybe, the heart is unvoiced but is voiced by the words. And there her journey started.

She loves spending time with herself and loves exploring new facts.

She thanks her parents that they supported her in her every dream and helped her in getting it true.

Contact her on:

Email Id: aashna.chawla11@gmail.com

Instagram Id: @unvoiced.heart

Yes we do!

 "Do you love her?" Asked his friend as he came and sat next to him .

The guy who was busy copying his assignment looked up in shock, "What are you saying? Who are you talking about?" He asked.

"I am talking about you. Do you love her?" He asked again. "I..i don't love her" He said.

"Stop faking it, we all know you guys are dating and are in love with eachother!" His friend said looking at her.

The girl who was helping out others with their assignments. "No we don't and I don't know what you are talking about!" Said the boy as he too looked at her. "I know dude. I'm your bestfriend and a bestfriend knows when the other one is in love or in an attraction and I even know the girl, come on!" His friend said and he looked down back at his assignment again.

"Buzz off or else I will kick you out, I have a lot of work to do and to complete!" He said as he again started working. "Whatever dude! I am also not free, I have a GIRLFRIEND and I accept it unlike people here." His friend said stressing the word ACCEPT.

And his friend walked out of the class. On the other hand her friend nudged her "Hey, can you give me your assignment?" And she was about to answer when her other friend replied "Oh! You are late, she gave her assignment to him. Don't you know? She is a full on lovergirl!"

Her friend mocked and all bursted out laughing except her who looked down. "Accept it, you love him, don't you ?" Asked her friend and she shook her head in a no. "No! I don't " She said.

"Everyone knows that you people love each other, stop ignoring commitments!" Her friends said. "No, we don't and moreover we don't talk" She said.

"And you concentrate on your assignment, or else I will leave. Then keep doing it all by yourself!" She warned . And all girls went silent. This always worked.

She looked at him and he looked up their eyes met.

And they looked away blushing where as A pen in his pocket & A locket around her neck smiled.

Because they again kept a secret.

Because some love stories are beautiful. Beautiful enough to be a secret,

Until they're tied in a forever, in a relationship named marriage.

TANYA VAID

1.

Sometimes, Not Saying Anything Is Saying A Lot. Silence is golden, but it can also be deafening. Some see silence as acceptance, others see it as a sign of wisdom, at the end of the day, silence will always hold a different meaning depending on situation.

Silence can be Painful, when all we want to do is hear back from someone who owns real estate in our heart, not having them respond, and not knowing what they're thinking can make us go mad. Silence can be loud, when horrible things are happening, and no one is speaking up, choosing to stay silent can make us accomplices. Silence can also open doors to the universe within us. When we're not speaking on the outside, that can enhance the conversation we're having on the inside. In this matter, silence can be our best friend. Sometimes, we feel the need to say something, then regret it immediately after.

Then we wish we stayed silent, but the vibrations we've sent out are already in the world, and we have to deal with those consequences. We'd be better off to remember to take our time when speaking on things that we feel strongly about, waiting a day will give us an opportunity to formulate our thoughts, and let emotions simmer. Let's pay more attention to our relationship with our silence, when it helps, and when it hurts. We can be saying so much during those moments we're saying nothing at All.

2.

We have Aspirations. Those aspirations may be anything from making rent, to owning a Ferrari for every day of the week. The specifics of our aspirations are irrelevant, actually our entire dream is pointless; if we don't plan on pulling that trigger & making it happen. We can do an awesome job sabotaging ourselves with excuses & reasons not to make things happen. Sometimes we trick ourselves into thinking we're going to make it happen "soon". Soon being "starting tomorrow, next week, next month, as soon as we have time, as soon as we have enough money, once our kids are grown". These abstract moments never arrive, but we feel like they will. In my experience, we just need to shut the f*ck up & START. No proclamations, no "as soon as..", no delays.

Just get started. Whatever we're afraid of, is dramatically worse in our mind, & that doesn't hold any weight in reality. Whatever great ideas we have are worthless, and pointless until they marry an execution (even in business, we can't copyright an idea, just the method of it's execution). The secret to success is not having a magical idea, but realizing that we are the key executioner that can't be copied if anyone tried. There is no one like us on this rock, there never was, and after We're gone, there won't be anyone like us again; that makes us 1 in 100 billion.

As that unique being, what can we accomplish & contribute during our limited moments on Earth? There are people accomplishing amazing things every day, Very little of it is luck. Most of it comes from a unfathomable amount of work that we rarely hear about. When we witness these accomplishments, we have a couple choices. We can drown in envy, & console ourselves with excuses as to why that can't be us (or even worse, why it shouldn't even be them). Or we can see their accomplishments as evidence that things beyond the norm are completely within our reach. We'll notice the pattern that most change comes from a change in our mind, before anything else in the outside world.

We don't need to know every step in our dreams, we just need to START. In 90 years we'll be dead anyways, what do WE really have to lose? Once we start moving; all those limitations & ideas of impossible fade. It's not going to be easy, but nothing worth accomplishing ever is. Most of my progress began the moment I began believing in myself more anyone else.

I have a feeling it'll be the same for us as Individually. No more excuses. Let's Identify What are our aspirations, & what are we going to do to get started?

NEHA MUTHREJA

1.Not everything you think is possible but not everything you decide is impossible

2.Things are inevitable if decisions are too

3.Thcy will ignore you if you will ignore yourself

4.Don't consider yourself inferior because how people see you depends on how you see yourself

5.If you want to be a candle to lighten up everyone's life Make sure you are ready to burn your happiness

6.Don't let a kid inside you die because an adult inside you can handle the world but not yourself

7.If failure is scary for you , you can never see the success in your life

8.If you want to be responsible in life take your life as a responsibility

9..Sometimes in search of better we leave the best

10.A person who only focuses on your flaws can never be called "yours"

11.It's not the darkness of problems it's the colour of courage that keeps us living

12.You notice reality when fakeness starts ignoring you

13.Disappointment fades when expectations too

14.Immaturity fades when responsibilities crosses path

15.If nothing is changing, try changing priorities

16.Live your life don't leave your life

17.Sometimes calmness is enough to break complexity

18.Decide wisely what you focus on because it blurs everything else

19.No journey of success begins without hope

20.It's your right to see dreams but it's your responsibility to fulfil it

21.How you behave when you are alone defines the real you

22.What makes you fall is your confidence What makes you rise is your confidence .

.

But what makes your confidence fall or rise is you.

KONKI KAMAL SHARON

Garbage into a blessing!

On a top of tree there are two parrots. Named chiko and pinko. Chiko asked pinko hey dude why are you so dull today what happened? Chiko when I was in return I alted on one building. There were happy shoutings I can notice they are in quite happy mood. After sometime there was pin drop silence over there. Just I have moved little forward onto window side. Total hall is filled with kids there faces was little happy and little sad. I thought it might be a hostel and they were scolded by warden. A small baby in the hands of a lady and she began this baby is new to our family and 5months old so we have to take care of her like a small little champ. Okay kids, she said. One of the kids asked mom who's she why's she here.

She didn't even have one year. From where did you bought this baby. One voice from back mom why again this baby have to suffer without parents if you weren't here to look after us how our lives used to end up. I thank God that she is 5months old when I came to this home I was one month old and I was thrown in a garbage. My beautiful roses listen to me you are the world's bestest creatures and you are God gifted kids but some people don't know the value of golden things untill they loose it. Okay tell me one thing if you have a home it will be filled with your parents and one sibling but here we are bound with more than one siblings. You can play, dance,study and build brightest futures under one shelter.

If you are not satisfied with this when you grow up adopt two elder people as your parents in that you can see your blessings. Can I get a brighter smiles on your faces. So can we welcome this little champ. They were overjoyed by seeing that little star. Chinko with teary eyes..Pinko it's really sadening part of the kids life but it's okay there are some people who are able to take care of them right. Don't trouble your heart we pray to God for them. As years passed exactly after 20years... On the same tree Pinko came little earlier and waiting for chinko. She came with over joyful and peaceful she looks. Arey chinko what's the matter you look so very happy what's the matter. Pinko do you know one thing. How come I will know arey a part from joking acha tell me what happened. Pinko asusual today I sat on the same tree where I used to sit.

Under that tree you know na I will listen different conversations. From past 1day the old couple sat overthere. I thought they were waiting for someone suddenly one girl came and asked them madam and sir where you are from? I have seen you last day too you are here with the same clothes. Have you searching for any address? Talk to me. What is your name amma the old people asked her Richa she said. Richa can you please say is there any old age home near to this place. Why amma Is there any one living there? No Richa we ourselves want to go there. My son thrown us out of home can you please give me the address. With teary eyes she asked why do you need this place only? They replied see Richa if my son doesn't love us we are loving him with all our heart if in any case he wanted us back we should available Richa that's why can u show us the route. Acha amma come with me I also followed them. They reached there. I was surprised the old people too. Richa it's not looking like an old age home it's looking like a home. Yeah you come in amma. Amma I don't know how my mom and dad was. I haven't seen them. I was born and left in a garbage and brought up by one wonderful lady in an orphan home I rather call it a blessed home. So my ma'am told me when you raise up if you find anyone left out take care of them give the love what you craved for years.

So on her knees she asked them can you be my parents for this life. Can you accept this proposal of mine. Can you allow me to call you amma and appa. They hugged her with joy and teary eyes. I don't know why your parents left you before but now I can say that God turned it into a blessing for many people lives. Today onwards we have one son and one daughter. Their happiness will not be replaced by anything else. Chinko is she the girl that I told you earlier. Yes she is. Pinko every thrown thing will turn into a blessing one day. This kid and two old people lives are true example of it. Indeed it's a big yes. May this blessings continue on every old age and orphan age homes. Garbagge stories will rock the country one day.

SHUBHAM SHAH

Love you to the moon and back.

A girl asked her boyfriend...

Babe.. you say always..." love you to moon and back..."

How much of it you mean..!!

The boy took a pause and began...

See my love...

My words might be cheesy, my sentences could seem doozy...

But my love !! My emotions! My time!! It is all I have for you. Every minute spent with you has been meaning full..!

Your smile defines the efforts I make...

You claim.. falling in love is all it takes...

But I differ.. From the time we met.. I began to hold myself and you… When you are low...

When you get irritated.. when you just seem to bang anything that steeps your way...I did all I could to calm you down! I started getting responsible...!!

You worked hard day and night... I was at ease.. carefree... But! my morning and night times changed..

Up-time from 1 in afternoon to morning 6... I started checking on someone's health..!!

Yeah... I began caring...!

I never felt like I was falling... you have been continuously improving me.!! As a matter of fact Unknowingly!!

I was rising... I just want you to be free...!!

A relationship where commitment is not just with talks... But the time invested together.!!

I wish you commit to complete faith in me.!! If we fall from the sky together...

U won't doubt getting hurt... If I say.. love you to the moon and back... Just Believe me…!

BHAVIKA JAIN

FAMILY COMES TOGETHER

Family Comes Together

For Always And Forever

In Sickness And In Health

In Poverty Or In Wealth

Family Comes Together

 For Always And Forever

Without Any Reason

Anytime Or Any Season

Family Comes Together

For Always And Forever

In Death Or In Life

In Happiness Or In Strife

Family Comes Together

For Always And Forever

In Anger Or In Kindness

Whether All Seeing Or In Blindness

Family Comes Together

For Always And Forever

Whether For Work Or For Play

They Somehow Find A Way

Family Comes Together

Because Families Are Forever....!!!!

SWOSTI MOHANTY

LOST

It's raining heavily. I dash towards a deserted building nearby that has already been a shelter to a stout man. I look around and see a black dog snarling at me.

Jeez...it's scary! This place seems totally unfamiliar to me. Which way to go now? I wonder. It's pouring cats and dogs. From a distance I see a discoloured board that had once been yellow, I think. It reads "Ajadganj, UP". What am I doing here? The last thing I remember is that I had had aloo paratha with tomato ketchup in a crowd. UP? How did I reach here? My goodness! I don't remember.

I can feel my stomach churning with fear. I swallow a lump in my throat and try to call my mommy. May be it's all a dreadful prank. My mom might just come out from behind this building and shout, "hey! You've been tricked!" But what if she doesn't? What if I am lost forever?

I try calling out for my mother. But I can't hear my voice! How can I not speak? I struggle to shout but it goes in vein. I give up. The air is chilly. I can hardly feel my legs anymore. If this cold breeze continues like this, I would certainly freeze. I take a deep breath and try to rearrange my thoughts. "Come on, Ira, think." I tell myself.

But before I could think something, I shudder at the weight of the man's hand on my shoulder. I break into a cold sweat. "Are you married?" He asks me.

"What an absurd question to be asked to a fifteen year old?" I think to myself. I want to say no but I can't find my voice. I try to slither away and pray to the heaven for the rain to stop. But the man won't give up. He again marches toward me and this time grabs me tightly.

Save me, O Heaven! I fidget and push him. However he seems to be a lot stronger than me and I end up falling on my back. Boom! I bang my face somewhere which I later realize is a marble floor.

I see a huge round face of a woman who tries to pick me up. Oh! Momma, I cry out of joy. My blanket was twisted around me like a python strangling its prey. "Why were you shouting – save me?" She demanded. "Oh! It's nothing. Sleep." I sighed.

SARITA SHUKLA (MILLIE)

1. On nights, when the sky

isn't sleepy enough,

the longing for your breath

comes to me like

the numb between heartbeats.

I'm reminded

of your fingers entwined with mine,

inseparably; of blinking dreams

that lay awake with us,

amidst fireflies — while our hearts

consummate their dilemmas.

On nights, when the sky isn't sleepy enough,

I sing too much of

the stars of dreams, the shores,

the tides, and the Moon.

Somewhere, all my metaphors

merge into you. The air on those nights,

smells only of anticipation;

my grounds await your ethereal touch.

Your eyes, become my mirror — on nights when the sky isn't sleepy enough..

2. With the chirruping of bird's, A gust of wind, a drop of rain A feeling of joy,

No feeling of pain Being a day dreamer, Soak the nature Soak the weather,

Let your soul float As light as feather, And the wanderlust Remains ✿

SUSMITA BISWAS

HOPE --- One Ray Of Happiness

Part 1:

It was the time of mid-January, Chilled breezes of the morning were touching her cheeks. She was gazing at the lake as if she was looking for something.

'Have you found anything?' an old man asked suddenly. 'I'm sorry. Have I just startled you?' he asked again.

'No. It's ok', she replied calmly. 'So, what are you searching for?' the old man asked again while sitting on the other side of the bench.

'I'm not searching for anything', she replied with annoyance. Then she stood up and started walking. 'Why does everyone not just leave me alone?' she muttered. Suddenly, she heard her name from behind. She stopped walking and turned around. It was Meghna, her best friend.

'Anita, I know you're upset, but you have to accept the fact. He cancelled the marriage, but it doesn't mean that your life has been ended. You have to love yourself. Think about your parents. They love you more than anyone else.' Meghna said to her.

'No, they don't. Otherwise, they would have never sent me to that place where everyone else is just abandoned like Me.', she cried loudly.

Part 2:

'Hope you will like this room.' the warden said to Anita. Anita said nothing and went close to the window as her parents were going back. A few drops of tears were rolled out on her cheeks but she wiped it out quickly. Then, suddenly her eyes fell on an old man and she was shocked. He was the same person with whom she met in the park yesterday. He was watering a plant of black roses!

She rushed down to him and asked, 'Why are you watering this plant?? Can't u see? There are so many beautiful flowers plants present here.' The old man replied gently, ' Yes there are many colorful flowers are present in this garden, but if you close your eyes and just touch every flower, you will feel that every flower is beautiful and this black one is softer than anyone else.' He continued, ' we often judge everything by just seeing them, we never try to feel their essence.' Anita was listening to him quietly, his words made her quite happy.

'Are you going to stay with us?' the old man asked.

'Yes, for just 30 days.' she answered.

'You can call me Mr. Sharma. We all live here together like a family. Come with me, I will introduce you to everyone', he said happily.

'No thanks. I am a bit tired now. I will meet them later.' Anita replied quickly and rushed to the upstairs.

'I have to stay here with these abandoned people for just 30 days and one day is almost passed.' she whispered while marking the date in the calendar.

The warden called her for dinner but she refused to come. She requested warden to give her dinner in her room. But, the warden told her that everyone had to abide by the rules of the house and she would have to sit down with everyone and eat dinner. When she entered the hall, she saw five people were sitting around a table, including Mr. Sharma. The warden introduced her to everyone.

'Such a lovely girl!' Madhu Ji, wife of Mr. Sharma, said and had invited Anita to sit beside her. Then she introduced everyone to Anita and they started dinner. Anita was so younger from all of them. But she started liking their conversation. She was trying to remember the last time she had spent with her parents like this. Because, for the last one year, she used to take her dinner in her room so that she could talk with her fiancé.

Gradually she started spending time with them; they used to cook food together, paint pictures, share stories of their lives and laugh together loudly. Anita began to believe in herself again. She often went to the garden with Mr. Sharma to help him watering the plants. His words had always been made her feel that the world is so big and there are so many beautiful things present in this world to experience.

Part 3:

One month had passed. Anita woke up in the morning and was watching the garden from her window; suddenly, she saw that the plant of black rose was almost bent onto the ground due to heavy rain of last night. She quickly went to the garden and tied the stem of the plant with a hard stick. She then touched the rose after closing her eyes. She felt like she touched her own heart. A few drops of tears again rolled out on her cheeks, but this time she felt better. The morning sun rays fell onto her face and after a long time she could feel the warmth of it. She felt the joy within herself. She looked beautiful just like nature, when the rays of the sun spread all around after a severe storm.

30 days had passed so quickly and she had come to know gradually that these people were not abandoned; rather they all had chosen this place to live for rest of their lives freely and happily. She had marked on the calendar and wrote "The beginning of a new journey".

A car had stopped outside the garden. It was Anita's parents and Meghna. They saw her. Anita had turned into a cheerful girl. Her eyes were sparkling with joy; they had seen the confidence into her eyes.

Anita bid goodbye to all. She hugged them like she used to always hug her grandparents. Their eyes were filled with tears, but they smiled looking to her. She came out of the garden and looked into the gate for the first time and read the line written over it: "**HOPE --- One Ray Of Happiness**".

NIKITA LABHANE

"Anjali." "Rahul",

" hey, I am not Rahul, I am Darshan, you idiot" He said irritatedly, "Why don't you change your name?, Anjali and Rahul sounds great" I said to piss him off, "Just shut up OHK, can't you think straight" he said, and dig under his pocket, taking out his IPhone, didn't I tell you, he is so addicted to this technical thing, "I guess you are born to use this gadget" I said, snatching his phone from his hand, he first glared me, I rolled my eyes, he looked at me with helpless eyes, "Anjali, yaar, listen ,tell Dad, I need some time" he said pleadingly, I chuckled, but then gave him serious look, "Tell him, that.. That.. You are dating someone" I said, he shook his head, "You know him, he will get it, I am lying" he replied, and yes he is right, after all our parents knows us better than anyone, "Actually, I have done something" he said, and I look at him suspiciously, I raised my eyebrows for his explanation,

"I told Dad, I like someone" he said, and my eyes widened, "WHAT?" I yelled, gaining unwanted attention from the people near us in cafe, "Can you keep your voice low, don't embarrass me" he hissed, I just rolled my eyes, "What did you say?, and how can he believe, who will say yes to you, you don't even have packs like sallu" I replied, laughing, he stare at me with love, what?, wait, no!, love! No way, I stopped abruptly,

 "I told him and he believed, and she loves me just because I don't have packs like Sallu, but a heart like Darshan" he winked at me, "He said, he wanna meet her, and ask her by himself" he said, and placed his hand over mine, "Don't tell me, I have to arrange a girl for you" I said offending, "No!, you don't, you just have to be with me" he replied. "You know she is hot, she is sexy, and... " " just shut up OHK, I mean I know I am your Best friend but I don't wanna listen about her" I said, removing my hand from his grip, "I need to use the washroom" I said, getting up, I took my large steps towards washroom, I closed the door, and just cry for a moment, I will loose my friend, my family, the only thing I have is him!, and now, he is also going away from him, I never had the courage to tell him,

How badly I have fallen in love with him, since the day he met me in kinder garden, my love just increased for him, I was knowing this day will come, when he will find his perfect match, and I will be left alone, again, anyways who love the girl who belongs to orphan, whose parents left her to someone else door, as she was a girl.

I cleaned my face, and move out of the washroom, I sat on the chair, where we were previously sitting, he is no where to be found, "Ma'am, your order" A waitress came, might be of my age, "I didn't pla--" I couldn't complete as she left keeping the order, I wondered what must be inside, curiosity takes in, I open the lid, and was shock to see the cake, my favorite, Dark Forest with lots of cherry on it!, but then I read 'For my Would be', ohh, she is mistaken its not our order, why Darshan will order this?, I am not his would be, "waiter"

I called a staff, "Its not our order" I said, tugging my loose strained of hair back, he smiled at me warmly, and indicated me to look at the stage, all lights were dim, and one focus falls on, 'Darshan', I look on to him, "Anjali, that's for you, I know I don't have packs like Sallu, but I can try to bring them out, you know 6 pack coming soon" he chuckled, making all others laugh along with him,

"I know what you think about me, you are thinking now I have started liking someone, I will ditch my best friend, you know na, now I have to give some time to her, to make her fall in love with me, and I wanna tell you one thing, its our last meeting" he said and paused, I looked at him with watery eyes, othat bitch!, so easily she snatched everything from me, "Because, after this, I would be meeting my girl friend, I want you to see her, and tell me how's my choice?"

He grin, I wanna run away somewhere, two people stand in front of me, Darshan came to me, and removed the cloth from whatever it is, he stood next to me, and I was having a confused look, it was mirror!, "So, how is she?, I wanna date her, and never wanna leave her, we look great with each other, aren't we?" He asked looking at our reflection in mirror, "Anjali, I can't be Rahul for you, but I can be 'your Darshan', forever and ever." he said. And "yes" escaped from my lips, I couldn't understand my feelings, he wants me, he pulled me in bear hug, his hugs are always precious for me,

"I told Dad, that we love each other, first he was shocked, but he smiled, and now, he want to know about your view on marrying with me, so, will you marry your kinder garden best friend?" He asked tilting his head, "No, he might have grown physically, but still he needs to attained kinder garden" I said ruffling his hair, all the cafe filled with claps, we cut the cake, and feed each other, love didn't change our friendship, but yes, it made it more stronger than before.

SUYASHI MISHRA

TITLE- A LOVE SONG FOR THE UNLOVED
(POEM)

Forests always intrigue me with their hard held secrets, and mysteries around them.

They proudly carry being disorganized, they don't plan . Plants just grow one upon another. So natural and raw, they are alive, free and boundless.

And you can never know them enough, just like your mind baby. It's beautiful, mysterious, and diverse, Just like the forest, which doesn't crave for order emancipates from predictability and what remains is weirdness , peculiarity, and eccentricity,

that you drink and swallow till it's last drop. It enchants me baby . To write a love song, on your being so untouched and pure, away from the usual. Flaunting your being not bits and fragments but the wholesome self. Frantically blessed as you are.

You show me life beyond constraints, as your energy knows no barrier. It calls for no steadiness, it enjoys being bumpy.

Just like forest knows no rules, no patterns; unaware and estranged as you are. Baby you probe me to come near as you push away through your darkness. You enchant, bewilder, and allure just like the forest you cast a spell, linger through my being appear in my dreams, and propel me to write,

To write a love song for you baby To sing soothing lullaby, when you have bad dreams, to kiss your forehead each night, and calm your being. Baby I fall for you each time

You surrender and fall asleep in my lap, vulnerable. I fall in love each time you call my name when you search me through the corridors. I fall in love when you look at me as if not seen from ages, Surround me with your arms, Smile, cry and laugh. You are a forest baby, and I am a wanderer .

Happen to discover you , When you didn't wish to be found. Each day I enter the mind of yours, to detangle fibres of your being. And make you embrace yourself, the way you embrace me cause you my baby are whole complete to an extent most of us can never be.

You taught me what books could never had. Baby I want you to know that you matter to me, and here's a love song for the one who loves without tricks and plans, without desires and demands.

For the one who trusts and shares their core with me, that others long for. My baby remember you are safe in my arms. You are beyond what anybody tells you. You are special.

And I love you unconditionally.

P.S.- Here love is profound care and affection towards someone in need of help. It is written from the perspective of a therapist/ caregiver for the marginalized section of our society, human beings with mental illnesses, to tell them although they are unloved by the society but there is someone who loves them.

VIBHA DESHPANDE

1. SWEET SURPRISE

The moment she saw him, she knew it was something that would change her forever

For she felt a stir in her tummy as though there were butterflies literally

It was all new to her- these feelings, these dreams

But she was ready to go on with it

One smile from him was what she longed for and her day was done

Little and sweet were her expectations

The silence between them made things exciting It was only in her mind that she was connected to him, his thoughts But reality was yet to be dawned upon

She had given herself to things like hope and dreams

Waiting for some magic to happen

One moment was what she waited for

She could not expect much though.

Little did she know that in a parallel universe

She was being someone's positive vibes every moment of the day

And also the sole reason that someone smiled-him.

2. DECISIONS

Sometimes you have to take hard decisions.

Which may hurt you now at the moment but that finallypays off later,

when you will realize that what you did was right after all.

On the way you hurt some people, you do crappy things but all that nullifies when the outcome is right.

You still will have a chance to win back those people who are meant to stay.

You even feel happy for doing those things so that it remains a part of your wonderful journey.

To choose between people or yourself is always hard, but it's up to us to decide.

Crashy paths on the go but the destination,

I bet will be worth all the hard work you did.

So be free to choose anything you love to do, no matter how difficult.

But always keep trying to work towards it and remember that it is most important to keep

Ourselves happy and only then we can spread smiles across, bright and deserving ones.

SHUBHAM KUMAR

1. The moment we start using pen by leaving our beloved pencil

We realize that it's not easy to erase our mistakes,

Neither go back to the time we have wasted...

2. I have the right words to complete my poetry,

But not the right person to complete my story.

NISHA SONI

1.

I'm sure, her lips were drop-dead gorgeous as her voice conveys alot about her.

The edges of her face shimmer in the light of haze highlight . its not only cover the bank but the nose perfectly, oh !! I really cherish the sharpness of the golden eye shadow when blinks.

She's shy and that's why the pink blush bounds her cheeks.

All over she's breathtaking but the editing of her eyes in the touch of mascara and waterline glam her thousand times.

Has gazzalinas of touch ups and I notice the limitations of her happiness. MAKEUP CAN COVER UP ALOT BUT IT CAN'T HIDE EVERYTHING

2.

Wondering of the old versions of mine so many

virtual reality combine

Pretending to move forward, get stuck in life's reward..

NOW

Keep observing the upcoming sight

I used to questioned myself day and night How irrelevant the order of delight ?

If supposed to the death next time.

SAGAR BHANDARE

I don't deny the fact that

I am void, I am nobody, I am worthless,

I have achieved nothing at all ,

I don't deserve to live at all but you know what I

I still believe in my dreams ,

I still feel that somehow i am gonna make it big , someday ;

Very soon i am gonna change the way people look at me .

 I am a cheater I cheat with my emotions.

I am a lier I lie to my heart. I am a killer I kill my ego for my friends .

I am a scientist I invent new ways to smile everyday.

I am a doctor I heal my pain by moving on. I am a writer I write what life shows.

I am a joker I entertain people. I am an idiot I believe everyone is my friend.

I am an optimist I hope for good . I am a pessimist I give up easily.

I am a hitchhiker I make everyone part of my journey.

I am Lucifer I made my life hell. I can't be a god Because for that I have to believe in myself first.

ANMOL PANDEY

A NEW MEMBER

"Hey!! Look, a new member just entered in our room" An old almira said.

"But it doesn't look so old or broken to be kept in a store room" An old chair replied. "But why he is so sad!"

Everyone who where in store room wondered. "Will you guys keep quite for a while" Oldest member of store room 'the mirror' scold them angrily' "Yes I'm sad", finally that picture frame, with a beautiful picture in it replied.

"I'm not only sad, but I'm hurt... I use to be staying beside there bed. Every time while sleeping, while entering into the room, at morning, they use to look at me with a smile, & why they not, after all I share there best memories, & was proof of love & chemistry between them, everyone get mesmerized when they look at me"

Then what went wrong, Y are you here now?? "Mirror asked politely" "Earlier, humans use to be emotional, they knew how to keep relationship working, But now, they are practical, they didn't even tried to resolve their issue, & left each other, & now they don't need me or this picture so they threw me here, &

I... I still remains same, with those mesmerizing memories, this loving picture but all alone" The frame keep telling... & his word were followed by unknown silence.

NATURE

Nature has its own way to teach us the lesson of life,

Yes it teach us, the way to survive. Autumn and Spring both are opposite to each other,

Like struggle & success are synonyms of one another. May beauty of nature fades away in autumn for a while,

But one should not forget that spring is there to keep it alive.

Just like seasons changes one by one, Time will definitely change have some patience.

Your happiness may fade away for a while, But definitely it will back & make you smile.

VILESHRANJITH

WHO IS A WRITER?

Someone who went through pain? Or the person who shares his pain?

Or the person who understands that pain..? Or maybe all of them..? I was confused and I am still.

Because I never expected myself to write, I never imagined people would exactly feel what I wrote...

I never thought of talking to writers who I don't even know.

All this just because I started writing randomly..? Who should I hold responsible for? Who caused pain..? Who helped me when I am in pain..? I don't know whether my writings makes sense when I started writing,

Because it was never written to make others feel, It was written to forget what I feel. I have many temporary people in my life, More than you can imagine. And I am used to it now, What am I used to...? Being used to being used.

You understand what I mean..? Yeah I am being mean... But who isn't in this temporary world When they get bored of you, When they have enough of you, They leave you, they abandon you.

And you start writing on them... Should you thank them..? Or should you wait for them to come back..? One thing is clear, That even if they come back, You won't stop writing. Once the writer comes out, he doesn't rest

He doesn't leave you Maybe it's good to not unlock him from the unexplored room.. Because once he is out, you get complicated, Your feelings become complicated You feel deep emotions, And sometimes this is a curse Of feeling every damn thing too deep Whether just some one ignoring you,

Or someone leaving you Yeah, I am being weird, But who isn't in this world? Your parents who love you but not your marks you get? (Not all) The friend who talks behind you? The two timing boy/girl friend? All of these have exception Because they are some people who are true But only lucky people get those Not all of us. Yeah, i am negative Because being positive always is foolish How is it you ask? Did the person you imagine to come back really came back..?

Hurting someone isn't positive Then why do people always do that? Temporary isn't temporary now for me, Temporary has become a permanent thing for me, It has built a house so strong that it won't leave, Temporary friends, temporary sadness and then comes temporary happiness And the loop goes on again and again,

Maybe the order changes but not the word TEMPORARY It's funny how people just stand with you one day And push you into a fiery pit the next day. This isn't the usual me, Because being nice to people is what I was teached to be, Making people laugh is what I decided to be, Because I found happiness there, Yeah I was selfish you see, Making people laugh for my own benefit. i smile a lot you know, Not because I am happy, Because I was sad for too long. I didn't like that long face I had. So what did I do?

I started finding smile in anything around me, Whether it's living or non-living. That's how I started liking to personify things. That's where I found happiness. Because nobody gave me the feeling of belongingness to me. And this is where I stop for now. Yours eversmiling unknown.

NIKITA MUKHERJEE

LIFE AFTER SCHOOL

When in school, we thought it wasn't so cool.

Morning prayers and going class in unison,

We were careless and had no outer connection.

School projects and assignments all around,

Time limit to finish all counts.

In Higher Secondary we thought of college.

All to be flowery and glossy with no restrictions.

But the truth was harsh,

Nobody will look upon you, who you are.

Life after school is really painful.

You need to focus, you need to be successful.

No spoon-feeding no pin-pointing on

BE WRONG

You need to understand yourself,

if you want to feel strong.

We eventually grow up in college, learn to accept brutal realities.

We learn the difference between playful childhood and

burden of responsibilities

We learn to accept our defeats

and improve ourselves for future.

We learn to behave with others

according to their nature.

We learn the difference between

childhood crush and serious relations.

There is a vital difference between our

expectation and reality of life.

Here we create our own path of success, we create our
individuality.

We cope up with all our problems without complaining.

We left our childish grumble and the habit of making fuss.

We grew up, we became mature and responsible

And above all we have learnt to love ourselves.

SHATAKSHI VASHISHTHA

To my love,

I would rather have a storm than the silent shores, I thought.

Something burning with fire and passion. Something so much more than me. Someone who has his dreams set and he would do anything for them.

Someone who winks at me anywhere and drives to my house at 2AM without thinking about the results.

Someoem who's reckless and lives in the moment.

Someone who is quick and quirky, who ditches parties to be with me.

I wanted adventure.

Something so strong that makes me feel like I'm the cosmos.

Then came he, he wouldn't grab my ass under a dinner table or kiss me in the middle of a street.

He'd rather curl up in a cold night alongside me.

He didn't read books and had dreams to talk about at the dawn, he'd his goals aimed.

So disciplined that he knew what he wants. He wouldn't get distracted, he wouldn't find excuses.

He had plans for five years and then ten.

He wouldn't rely on anyone but him.

He didn't talk to my dad about his favorite politician or kissed my mom's cheek, he would silently nod and pass a small smile before holding hands with me.

He was a wreck.

He said, it's cliché the concept of love at first sight but you took my damn breath away.

He wouldn't braid my hair or paint with me but he'd share his fries and coke with me.

He didn't give much thought about the characters in a movie and when the movie ends, it'd ended for him but it didn't for me.He would hold me in days of anxiety and nervousness.

Leave his laptop and endless paper work chaos just to give a shoulder massage on my cranky days of periods.

He said he's not the kind of guy I write poems about but he doesn't knows he's the kind of guy why I'm still able to write poems about various subjects

He's smart and he's a wreck, he's careless but so responsible.

He knows all my looks and what do they mean, he knows when to hold me and when to let me go.

He said, I don't think about others, others dreams and desires but I want yours and only yours to come true.

He knows so much about me I thought no one will ever come know.

He is this adorable baby some days, and someday he's full of faith in every little thing. He's beautiful for anything and everything he's, without even realizing.

He thinks his personality is dull but all I see when I look at him is, my light.

He's silly and and never fails to make me laugh.

He's restless until his work is done which makes him so irresistibly attractive, I hope he knows.

He's brave and he makes me feel so safe.

May I be anywhere in this world but he...he would make me feel I'm home, in his arms curled.

And he's flawed, too flawed which makes him perfect.

He has issues and he gets mad but I love him.

He's the man I love and I'd ditch a thousand adventures to be a part with him in his legacy.

I think I wanted the storm but I'd rather have the calm night that comes after it, I just hope he knows.

RK NATHAN

Ananya- There is a young girl by the name Deepika living in a caves of Sarva Mountains. It is not llike an ordinary mountain. The cave is at the center inside of the mountain. There she is doing Shiva Pooja since many yugas. She never comes out of the mountain. But every day after 2:00 AM she goes to the the nearby lake which was known as Padma Poorva The lake is fully covered with Lotus) to take bath and get water and flowers for the shiva pooja There was a inner tunnel which connects the cave to the lake. There under the lake a Devi Temple. The name of the devi is Vriddha. She is holding a magical music instrument. There is also a secret room under the idol of devi. If secret music note (password like) played using the instrument the door of the secret room get opened. The secret room filled with divine aroma there she takes bath and dresses up. Before 4:45 AM she goes back to the cave.

Through out the day she does Shiva Pooja. One day she had erotic dream after that night the next 7 days she couldn't get up from the sleep. One day the hero of this story falling from the sky.He falls on the lake Padma Poorva. After he touches the water of Padma Poorva he become ashes. After 7 days deepika getting up from the sleep. She forgot about the dream. Again she started doing her routine work. As usual she went to Devi temple. There she saw the beautiful butterfly. While she is watching the butterfly stated growing within few minutes it grown like a giant. That butterfly started talking to her. It asked her do you want to have a ride I will show you the entire world. She said yes but we have to return within a day. It said okay. After many yugas she is coming out from the mountains. She enjoyed the beautiful world. Then the butterfly left her in the the lake. The friend ship continued with fun and entertainment. One day she was in riding the butterfly. An eagle kidnapped the Deepika. It reached a domain in the space named as Varaha Garbha. Here is our villain named Varahan. He was proposing the sex favour to her.She said look Varahan what do you think of me iam already having a guy. Not only today daily you can have a sex with me I can able to give you the ultimate pleasure for that you have to kill my guy. The sad thing is I don't know where he has gone. One day he will come if he come he will finishes you because he is very strong man. Varahan agreed to kill her guy.He arrested in the jail. He searched in all universe. He couldn't find. Later he came to know that she lied. He went to the jail with the intension of rape her. But there she was missing. The very next he put in the jail. The butterfly rescued her from there. He become very angry And came to the bank of Padma Poorva. There she was talking with the butterfly. On seeing her she become very anger. He was trying to attack her. The butterfly took the giant form and started protecting her. He become tired . He touches the water of Padma Poorva to take some water. Suddenly a soldier came from the lake. The butterfly scared after seeing the soldier. Suddenly he took the sword and cut the wings of the butterfly. Varahan become happy on the seeing the death of butterfly. The soldier saw the girl and gave a her a sarcastic smile.

Actually she was stunned on seeing the action of the soldier. Oh Varaha because of your touch I have got my original form. Tell me Varaha what can I give as a token of compliment. Varaha said oh my dear friend thank you so much I need that girl. I wanna rape her just go and get her. He dragged the girl and handed over to Varaha. Varaha was going to remove her dress. He just raised his hand. Suddenly his head has been cut by the sword of the soldier. She become statue for a minute. Someone sprayed the water on her face. Again she become stunned because the butterfly spraying the water with the wings. She cannot guess whats happening. The soldier started to explain that…

Part 2 SOON..

Varaha was my enemy I cannot defeat him in his domain. He sexually assaulted my lady love. At that time I was powerless and hopeless. Even though I went to fight he kicked me out of his kingdom. I fell on this Padma Poorva after touching this holy water I got more divine strength. She thanked him and asked his name. He said that Vridhakasi belong to the domain Padma Garbha. She took him to the underwater Devi temple and to the secret room also. They are sitting together and talking to each other and playing. Suddenly there was a earthquake which resulted in love quake in each other. They started exchanging their love through the outer medium of the inner spirit. Unconditionally they had sex. She left him there and went to the mountain to pay thanks and prayer to Shiva for giving her Vridhakasi. While she was thanking Shiva she heard the voice of Vridhakasi.

She went to the Devi temple and she came up above the water. A terrific girl taking him in the Space ship. At once she called her butterfly friend. It carried her and started chasing the space ship. At one point the butterfly unable to fly. The wing become motionless and become falling from the space. He shouted the name of Vayu Bagawan. Suddenly a big golden plate came from somewhere.They fall on the golden plate. The plate took them to the Saravana Gharba. There they met Charvadhan. He has four lady partners. They welcome them and fed them. Deepika explained what happened. He promised that he will help them. He looked at his four ladies the four become one and Charvadhan become a dual weapon in her hand. From now she is named as

Charvadhanaa. Charvadhanaa rotated the weapon in the air. It found the direction of the space ship and the weapon informed her the space ship is in Gaja Garbha. After hearing this there was silence in her face. Because Gaja Garbha is the chief garbha of all divine garbha. The matter become so serious. The one become four again. The weapon become Charvadhan. He sat with sorrow. The butterfly started laughing.

All were looking the butterfly. The butterfly revealed the truth. I am the master mind in this kidnap sequence. She is none other than Vridhakasi 's lady love Baladehi. The next moment the butterfly disappeared from there. They cannot imagine the situation what they are facing. Then the butterfly entered in to the Gaja Garbha. Everyone is paying heartful respect to the butterfly. The Gaja Indira started praising the butterfly with the utmost devotion. Who is the Butterfly which is receiving royal respect from all the king of all domains.

ASTHA YADAV

WHEN LOVE ENTERS

What an immensely beautiful feeling,

the world changes, person changes

and most probably for good.

When true partner and true love enters,

it actually makes a person good.

It is a magic,

It motivates,

It makes you believe,

It makes you jealous,

It makes you act like kid,

It makes you feel other emotions,

It makes you a positive thinker,

It boosts your morale,

It makes you take your life seriously,

It makes you happy,

It makes you sad sometimes,

It makes you kind,

It makes you crazy in positively cute manner,

It in fact is magical.

ENDING IT WAS THE RIGHT TIIING TO DO.

After ending our 4 year relationship, I went to meet him for the last time and finally here we are , staring at each other as strangers, either of us unsure of what to say.

Maintaining that long distance relationship for 4 years, was not easy at all. We laughed everyday with or on each other during video calls. Despite being away, messages from him made me feel less alone.

I miss the conversation we used to have. Sometimes I miss how I didn't have to explain him anything. Cutting contact with him was hard because he had become a constant.

I remember sitting on the cold bathroom floor with tears rolling down my cheeks. But ending it was the right thing to do before it was taken to a place where I couldn't look back on our time together and smile despite the ending.

PRANJAL BISHT

Tell me, please. As sound as her breathing was just as the wind flowing making the leaves flutter slightly announcing the arrival of fall. Wind being a bit chilly as she dipped her hands deep in the pockets of her jeans. She most felt the winters rather any season. Sun was moderately shining soothing the chill as she head towards his home with all hopes of him not being there. She has planned it since ages and didn't want it to be ruined at any cost. She was excitedly nervous and it showed on her face. Just as she stepped out of the elevator which stopped at 10th floor sliding the keys and unlocked the door. Relief filled her nerves as his presence was not felt. One year has passed since they have been together. Togetherness past bads. Togetherness past lows. Since she recovered. She locked the doors and started preparing to surprise him.

It's not like it was the best surprise she could ever give him but still she didn't want to leave a special day like this. The memory of his holding her week hands for the first time and asking her out was still fresh in her mind. They were poles apart. Him being a lazy ass and messy as she was always punctual about everything and so organised. But as they say opposite attracts, so did they. As much as she loved him she never thought she could love someone more than her breath. She pulled her hairs up in a bun on the top of her head and started cleaning up the regular mess that shows up in his apartment. She picked his clothes and set them inside the washer. Picked the bedsheets and changed them with new ones, opening the curtains allowing the sunlight in the room.

She lighted the candles as the sent filled the room claming her nerves. She shifted to the drawers that were half open and opened them up setting them up neatly only to find the unexpected. The post card pictures seemed unfamiliar and she didn't remember any such photographs of them together. As she took a closer look her mind instinctively backed off not accepting what her eyes saw. Her heart did skip a beat and her pulse quickened. Beneath the pictures laid a cell phone. It was not his and she knew it. She switched it on and the home screen appears and she straight went to the gallery and there it was. A whole goddamned video of her making love with him. She trusted him so much and this is what he does with the trust she provided him. Tears fell down not accepting what she just saw as the door cracks open and he came with full grin on his face. "Hey I didn't knew..." his voice trails off at the sight of her cheeks strained with tears.

Her fists clenched the picture as she threw the cell phone on the ground ensuring it would turn in pieces as she strommed off the bed room down in the hallway when his strong hands gripped around her arms stopping her mid way. "Don't you date touch me with those filthy hands of yours" she shouted and jerked off his hands freeing her arms. Whipping off her tears with the back of her hands she ran out of his apartment "Riya listen to me..." she could hear his words somewhere far and she didn't know where she was going. Her legs gave up and she found herself on the terrace. She ran all the way up there and her lungs gave out draining her whole energy as she heard his steps closer and she stoop up and on the railing with the pictures still clenched in her hands. "What did i ever do to deserve you, Vihan." She said as she saw him coming closer to her, her voice submerging the sound of wind. She stood there her hands gesturing to stop him from coming any forward. "Why would you do this to me?" She said, tears pooling in her eyes threatening to escape again. "Look riya, you need to come down right now. What you're doing is stupid." Vihan shouted.

"The stupidest thing I've ever done is to love you, to trust you Vihan." She said "Did you enjoy the video you made of me? Huh? Showing it to the world to destroy my life!" Tears now flowing. "Riya I'm sorry. I'm sorry for whatever I've done. I'm sorry i broke your trust but...but please come down. Please I love you...i really do "His voice cracked as he said those words as if...as if he was going to break down.

"I should've died the day I tried to save you from that dammed truck" she stated as her hairs swayed with the wind "After all that I've done for you, you repay me with this.." she says throwing the pictures, her voice almost a whisper and agony takes over. Riya closes her eyes and let the gravity rule her. Her body feeling lighter after every passing second and he ran towards the railing. "NO..." a shriek escapes his lips as she fell on the green mattress. "Cut. Okay. Well done!!" the director squeak as everyone applauded the actors.

Smrita stood on her feet and bowed down to everyone thanking as Shohid came to hug her "Semmed like a major déjà vu" he whispered as chills ran down her spine. "What did I seriously do to ever deserve you Shohid" Smtita said eye in his eye as his smirk grew wider.

TANNU JHA

He's not fire,

But he still ravages me.

He's not wind,

But he makes me fly.

He's not water,

But I still drown in him.

He's something much deeper, I

just don't know what yet.

ARYA ARTIS

A PAGE FROM BACK BENCHERS DIARY

A The great Scientist Albert Einstein once said and I quote"Everybody is a genius But if you judge a fish by its ability to climb a tree, it will live it's whole life belicving that it is stupid". The education system out here treats me as the clownfish NEMO lost in the Great Barrier Reef.

A good morning, to all the teachers, intellectuals, scholars and my so called relatives and neighbours who advertise a caring attitude towards me. It's been 12 years for me to get on a daily routine, for waking up and marching my way towards the school. I will have to face my Board exams till the time this hand written piece reaches out to you. I have been a constant BackBencher since my kindergarten days, being a Backbencher has always helped me to emphasise others feeling very well.

We Backbenchers never complained about the teachers or any wrong macula towards us, but I would like to add on that in each class there is a cricketer whose physics doesn't matter, in each class there is a singer whose mathematical ability to solve problems doesn't matter. We Backbenchers too fall in love but our feelings are suppressed in the burden of RD SHARMA and a ballast of text books.

People mock at us just because we are unable to mcmorise those few pages to be puked in the answer sheet. We still gather guts and walk up daily to those moth- eaten rooms just to glance a smile from our parents. Being a Backbencher my words will be shush and will be trolled for my English but I hope my words will give voice to all those Backbenchers out there.

PREM KUMAR

58

1. "Are we really sure"

Something that she long for

Is right in front of her .

When you look it everyday

you don't have to chase it

But you close it anyway .

Ever wondered why hands got cold?

Why you skip your heart beat ?

You have to step behind

Even if you really mean it .

You'd rather try to hide it

Deep beneath your smile ,

Won't let it bloom like flower

In the open even if it's just for a while .

Because it deep hurts to let go of

Something incredible and pure .

Would you ever recover from the loss .

I'm afraid we are sure !

2. "Wishes"

You know we all did things

We wished but we didn't .

 And then there are moments

we wish we did but we couldn't .

3. "Story"

His life's best story was not written

with pen it was always she who wrote it with her kajal .

4. "Tenses"

She explained me the importance of tense and

I realized it when 'e' in her 'love' changed to 'ed' .

DIPIKA GOUDA

SIMILAR SITUATION

Life begins when we take birth

But what is the basis for being on earth?

Time passes and here arrives the childhood station

Which lead us to career and our education.

Following the usual path yet others want to win the world,

Some have talent besides others believe in what they have learned.

Being simple and innocent is a challenge,

But somehow we all manage.

Competition,the only word which clicks in out minds,

But friendship is something that binds.

 Age is just a number Although death is ultimate,that bothers.

As I am fearless just like a lioness And that's the reason,

I live life to the fullest.

NEW ME EVERYDAY

When darkness prevails all around that's the time when I wake up.

Thinking about what lacks in my life , realising it with a close up.

Is having a dream or an ambition not enough?

Well, being in this situation is tough.

It's like working hard to go beneath the sea and found sand everywhere.

Surely my life is playing with me, a dare.

Love and affection is all I need to console myself, which is way more essential than wealth.

Small heart dreaming for a great thing to happen,

Yet my eyes know what is my passion.

People breaking my heart like mirror but I can still see my face without an error.

RIDDHI UPADHYAY

Lets romantisize pain, Flirt with scars of each other.

Kiss the darkest days of our, together.

Lets hymn the agonies of our past To make from it, the best song of our lives.

Admist the immposibilties of us,

Lets dream of an empire together.

Fill the cracks between our soul With intimacy of thoughts and certainity.

Adorn it with our smiles and little love bites.

Lets be the love to each other we always wanted!

Don't you dare to fall for What I look...

Fall for what is hidden in me. Fall for my scars,

Fall for my wounds I'm carrying from ages, Fall for my bleeding heart,

Fall for my broken pieces I'm left with, Fall for my blood tears,

Fall for my agony , Fall for my blue days, Fall for my torn soul,

Fall for me when I become anagapesis, Fall for all what I never show you,

Don't just fall rather grow with me... In love

PRAHARSHA ISRUPU

BEING INTROVERT

An introvert is the one who can hide a lot of emotions but still could maintain a smile on their face.

An introvert is the one who carries an ocean in their heart but still choose to be sielent.

An introvert will be the one who thinks twice before giving replies cause they are concernèd abt how the other feels.

An introvert choose to be silent not because they are not understood by anyone, its just because they don't want to socialise their things.

An introvert is the one who may cry for an hour inside a room and still come out with a big smile on their face.

An introvert can survive without anything alone in a room and still be happy.

They say that it needs a lot of courage to be an "extrovert" and to express everything, but in reality introverts need more courage to just hide everything with a smile.

Being an introvert you need to face a lot of criticisms.

People say that "you are stingy".

But who knows that it's just your personality to choose silence over chaos.

But the worst part of being an introvert is bearing an untold story inside you.

TASMAYEE BISWAL

AM I THE ONE?

Am I The One? Am I the one standing all alone,

With all the possible hazards,

Happening all around me?

Cause suffering is what I know.

The toughest of all was, walking,

With the fire in the heart, that

Has also stopped burning, cause,

The flames have also become tired.

It hurts to see people smiling,

On their own faults, without,

Even knowing that, they,

Are going to regret later!

Am I the only one,

Regretting for my mistakes?

CAFFEINATED PAGES

Cause they had made a lot,

But never felt guilty of that.

The toughest of all was, making

Decisions that were always wrong,

But never were made correct,

That seemed to be upsetting.

It hurts to know that, some

 Hopes will never be true

Still you keep them, expecting,

They may once become true.

Am I the one standing alone,

With all those pain in the heart,

Tearing me always apart?

Cause, they can't be smiled at.

NAVRANG DAMODAR

Leave:

No matter how much I tried to convince you , But you were so determined , so eager that you had just turned deaf to my words.

Rain:

Sporadic and intermittent monsoon rain due to the nimbostratus cloud still reminds me of the rainy day, standing in front of the college under the showering nature of a rain , when I had held your hand, not inadvertently but just because I never wanted you to leave me and put me into an unwanted isolation forever.

Angel:

We can never be friends again on the earth. But I wish to see you in heaven, for I want to see you as an Angel And myself as a crown That you wear on your head With the pride in your heart. I like the way you shut me up, then I don't speak anything for another three days just keep thinking how you do it. I hate people who lie, but when its you who lie, I just try to compromise with my values. Don't come back I am busy in loving you.

5. I will never hurt someone

I will never hurt someone because you taught me how it feels to get hurt, I will never leave someone because you taught me how It feels in isolation, I will always support another person because you taught me how it feels when there is nobody to support you and encourage you, I will never make someone wait for me because you taught me how it feels to wait for someone for hours, I will never expect anything from others because you taught me how it feels when your expectations are left unfulfilled,

6. Promises:

It was so easy for you to make promises, Very hard for me to do the same for you mrs, Without informing you, I often left your sight, Having full faith that you will always be with it abide, but you surprisingly proved me wrong , By breaking the promises that you had kept for so long, your promises on my soul have now become an old bruise, Certainly I had forgotten that it was not a binding truce, but now I think what if it was an agreement, you would never have left me like a Kareena in jab we met, But now I take pride in the thing that I did not promise the same, failing to keep it, would have made me feel very ashamed, You made me realise that my opinion should not be reformed, cause it is always better to under promise and over perform. It's been a long time and it still feels like I cannot survive without you as if you have used some spell to subjugate me . Sometimes I wake up, I wake up just to realise that you have left,

\

TANYA SEN

1. Forever Asleep

I want to rip my heart off,

But I know I'm falling in deep.

I want to wake up from this dream,

Before I am forever asleep.

2. Please Stay...

I'll hold your hand till it goes cold,

My heart will beat for your soul,

It's neither stars nor the shore,

It's just you that makes me whole.

In the ocean I would've drowned,

If it's you that I would've found,

Why in my chest echoes your heartbeat's sound?

But I know this life is a maze that goes around.

But still with the tears that won't ever cease,

CAFFEINATED PAGES

Anything my heart won't feel,

With my last hope of you to heal,

I'll ask, is it important for you to leave?

Please stay...

PREETI BISWAS

Dear inter religion love,

"Some words don't merge. Be careful." No doubt my love, you were correct. I denied the truth in search of illusion.

The latter slipped from my hands, as sand does and like you.

I merged the meaning of our names.To give you a nickname. You loved it. I wonder if you still do !!

Love and togetherness - the nickname meant. But we were never meant to be.

Had our fate merged instead of names, it would have been more beautiful

We can either be together or be in love. The way we existed before.

Two individuals, each of us meaning love and togetherness, respectively.

The cold winter nights, glued to the phones, talking endlessly of how

I write poems on you and you are a part of my everyday diary. You called it love. I denied every single time. I meant the opposite.

 I confessed you rejected. All in poems never in real.

One not so fine day, you informed about your nikaah. Until then I never felt, what people called pain. Left the coffee half drunk, my favourite addiction. Count yourself prior to that please.

Engagement the next year. A couple of month to this year's departure. I should consider myself too. You told why you never wanted me to fall for you. " I don't see a future with you. I cannot accept you, but don't want to reject you."

The maze of confusion kept on colliding endlessly.

My friends told you love me. You're a writer as well and your poems explicitly showed the same. You told a different story though. Everytime I asked, you replied a clear no. I pretended the same. Either of us knew that it's not true.

Neither of us accepting the same. Maybe in a fear.

Both of us knew, we loved each other. Just never confessed.

Are you scared of falling too hard, to detach yourself from me, if the future brings a denial ??

Should I say, you already fell. I've seen love in your eyes, the way you look at me.

The way you speak to me, each word departing from your lips carry a love, unaffected by society's norms.

 Every time you said you don't love me, your eyes never met mine. Can I ask the reason please ?

Don't tell me you love me too. And we cannot be together.

The only reason why you never confess. Why you play a different rude character of you, everytime I talk of love ?

I keep scrounging for answers I will never get.

Perhaps we were two parallel lines, moving in the same direction, intersected once by chance and diverted with a greater force.

I still wait for you, in the horizon, where miracles happen. Someday when it's not a sin to love someone from different religion.

Come to me and say, Yes I love you. I shall reply, I love you too, my love.

Let's take a walk to heaven. The world wouldn't accept pure love, until religion is embedded in it's narrow mindset.

We shall then fly to sky, freeing ourselves, from the shackles, and taunts I've been receiving my all life. 'Being a Hindu how can you marry a Muslim.'

Let's leave my love. A new world is waiting.

Yours,

 Inter religion love, who never confessed for the societal fear.

ANKUR SACHAN

1. Yes you are my favourite dream book, I can read you without opening you up. I don't need roses for the smell of book, the care you've for me is the fragrance enough, the way you hold me up with confidence makes me the most important line of your favourite book and your hug to me is same as adding up more such beautiful lines to this book of our love.

2. After blocking you in my arms, After locking you in my heart. The feelings is of painting unbreakable promises on your soul with the color of my passion for you. And I want to paint this painting every moment of my life with our color I want you to be the last stroke of my every painting that completes it.

3. Hug me in the morning from behind and whisper all those fantasies I told you yesterday night, because I'll make it my today's goal.

4. "Hey, How are you?, I love you." She texted. "I miss you." He replied crying. Miss you texts are way more affective than I love you ones.

5. My self esteem is my confidence.

My self esteem is my confidence.

I feel that if I compromised my self esteem then I will become weak.

So I will never compromise with self esteem.

My deal with self-esteem will tell me every moment of my life that at some time I was so weak.

I have compromised with my self-esteem, I do not want to feel this weakness again and again.

If I compromised once with my self esteem, it would mean that I killed my self belief forever.

And I will never be able to feel it so firmly. My self esteem is that part of my life which gives me the confidence of having a strong side in front of others.

My self-respect gives me the freedom that I feel myself strong.

My self esteem gives me strong confidence in taking big decisions.

I will not change my self esteem with stubbornness.

But I will never make any compromise with it for a moment.

SHUBHAM JAIN

1. My Love

For You My love for you is so intense that,

I would write you always on your favourite star you see at night

2. Smile

A precious gift from God, with which you can change the world,

but don't let the world change your smile

SAHIL SOURAV

Ever failed miserably in life ?

Obviously your answer would be a big yes! After all we aren't super humans. You might have experienced once when we start failing, everything starts backfiring. No plans get executed and accomplishment of it seems like a fish out of water. Constant failures surrounds us and keeps enervating and breaking us from within bit by bit untill we're completely shattered and ready to give up. And if you try too hard, it ends up in a farrago, surrounded by a gall of sadness. I know you felt that (I'm too a human being).

Sometimes delusions can be so frightening. You're aiming for something big and suddenly you fall from an unmeasurable height. And in a split, everything's gone. Suppressions, annexations and fear entraps us in a bubble of frustration and we eventually succumb to it. Some keep lamenting on what went wrong and ultimately everything comes to a standstill. A deadlock that seems unbreakable.Not knowing what to do, where to start from. It becomes an intricate task. But I'm sorry if you're expecting any remedies because I too have become a regular customer of "MR. FAILURE"(kidding). We're so obsessed with failures and stories related to it that we don't even try to push ourselves.

If someone hurts you, don't you think of vengeance? Then why not with failure? "Mr. Failure" throws a gauntlet at us and we simply back down even without putting our honest effort and trying. Nothing ends when you fail, actually it all starts then and there itself. Unless you fail, can you become a perfect human being ? Failures are a part of life and they are the reason for your perfection. If you don't fail, what story would you be telling to your grandchildren of your struggle with failure? I'm sure you would be happy when they find a source of motivation in you and not Mr. Sandeep Maheshwari. The only thing I can say is you can be a winner or a loser, all depends on you and your mindset.

The small failures you think that ruined you, are the loop holes for more bigger and drastic ones. . Discover your afflictions and most importantly rectify them. Never back down due to fear of failing. Take your time and keep absorbing positivity, you might fail a numerous times but the victory after it would surely pump your spirits higher than the Everest.

 Learn to accept challenges, no matter what would be the end result.

You have it in you and nobody can stop it. You are the best. Believe that and keep fighting.

ISHAN NIMDEOKAR

1. Abundance of Wishes!! With oodles of things you own

To Plenitude of things you desire

Puts me in state of confusion,

While having abundant wishes to plead,

Why don't you get it, when they reach.

Objects enclosing you are insignificant,

Than stuffs out of its circumference

Materials employed to write against materiality,

Though you need them still you oppose their necessity.

Facts provide, man with mind

Repudiate things at a wild

To collect what he want,

To assuage his untold wants.

2. An illuminating flameMakes me exclaim

Being burning

What it gains,

It says undoubtedly

Spreading brightness

Brings me reason,

As my end is fasten

Till then let me lighten

To enlighten the dejected souls,

 Instead of getting into fire

Just set me, fire of glow

Which expeditiously could blow

To uproot the gloomy layer

When I put to go..

NIDHI SUGANDH

1. Hair gets Lighter,

Skin gets Darker,

Summer's be back!!

Summer's be back !!

Exam get's over,

Music becomes louder,

Summer's be back!!

Summer's be back!!

 Air gets warmer,

Drink gets colder,

Summer's be back !!

Summer's be back !!

2. " Decide Today"

Decide, Today

Decide your worth.

Decide what you look good in,

Happiness and strength,

OR

Tears and hurt.

Decide, what you wish to do today ,

Plan and work on your dream,

OR

Sit and complain about the present situation.

Decide , Today whether you want to impress people,

OR

Inspire people.

Decide Today, Because Today is the day.

DEEPSHIKHA AGARWAL

1. A LOVELY WARNING

Hey Sleep on time, Hey Wake up early! Hey Concentrate on your studies,

Hey Keep Quite she is my love! Hey You've no right to blame her, Hey She is my world!

Hey She is my world, Hey She is my everything!

No one has any right to say anything to her, No one has any right to claim her!

She is love forever, Hey Be Beautiful! Hey keep your success ongoing,

Now it's a warning keep your phone and sleep! Go sleep and sleep well, You have to wake up early tomorrow! You're my darling and you should be the best,

You should never be regretting about what you do in any situation! Remember you have to be the best, Remember you are the crown of my head!

Sleep! Sleep! Sleep! Now go to sleep! Common keep the phone aside,

Common keep the books asise!

All these warnings from childhood till the day of my Marriage, Were never warnings but the care and concern of a father

THESE ALL WARNINGS ARE THE PURE LOVE OF A FATHER FOR HIS BELOVED DAUGHTER

YES EVERY SINGLE DAUGHTER IS BLESSED TO LISTEN ALL THESE WONDERFUL AND LOVELY WARNINGS FROM THE LOVE OF THEIR LIFE-THEIR FATHER

2. Responsibility It is your responsibility to see that you are respected,

It is you who are responsible for whatever happens with you!

When you complete all your responsibilities correctly,

You get respected in the society!

It's your moral responsibility to see everyone is treated equally,

It's your moral responsibility seeking respect for yourself and everyone!

It's your responsibility to choose a correct candidate as your representative,

It's your responsibility to see whether you are going on the correct path or not!

Being a person it's your responsibility to make everyone satisfied,

Being a part of society it's your responsibility to see everyone is safe!

Being a part of your family it's your responsibility to see that Noone is sad or unhappy,

Being the leader of the team it's your responsibility to make each other comfortable and also work like a team!

It's your responsibility as a caption to take perfect decisions and make everyone lead towards success and unity! It's your responsibility as a teacher to guide your students perfectly,

It's your responsibility as parents to fulfil all the needs and wants of your child but also to look that they don't choose the wrong path!

It's your responsibility to seek help from the ones who know,

It's your responsibility to help the ones who need you!

As a person it's your responsibility to make everyone happy,

 As a person it's your responsibility to make a different and happy place to live in for all!

First you have to fulfil all your responsibilities and then only you would be able to survive in a better way,

First live upto the expectations of others complete all your responsibilities then only you will be able to lead a peaceful life!

SUBHODEEP PRAMANIK

1. The day you left, ever after I tried penning down my feelings; connecting the alphabets; the words bleeded your memories.

2. Sudden change from treacherous heat,

   To delightful mild temperature

   From hot suffering winds,

   To pleasing cold breeze

   From running inside the shelters away from sun,

   To coming out of house to enjoy weather

   Dusk is reward of God,

   For surviving the day

3. The rose was so jealous; when he embarrassed her and was lost in her prepossessing, while holding the most beautiful flower(rose) in his hand which was ignored in front of her alluring charm.

4. The day, the rose lost all it's arrogance; when he used it to propose an undecorated soul, and she refused it.Love was first turning point of his life., Then he never saw a straight road again.

5. He loved her soul, instead of her body. So the scars she left was only on his soul. She was broken and scattered into pieces. He collected the pieces and made the most beautiful collage. Empty pockets, isolations, misfortunes, sad past and broken hearts are optimum conditions to become a writer.

SAFIYA MOTIWALA

1. My daughter

You are a pretty little princess

With sparkling bright eyes;

You possess a golden heart

Like angels in the skies!

I love your innocent smile,

I adore your gentle voice

I cherish the moments spent with you

Oh! They make my heart rejoice.

If I ever had a magic wand

The only wish from my heart

Would be to stay with you forever

And never let you part.

2. The koel

CAFFEINATED PAGES

In the oppressive heat of summer

Her melody soothes my heart;

I eagerly wait for the heavenly music

When my day is about to start.

Always hidden behind the boughs

I wish she would let me see;

I fall for her enchanting voice

It fills me up with glee!

91

BIO AND PICTURES OF CO-AUTHORS

Tanya Vaid,a girl with ambitions in her eyes,survived in multiple cities.And a power pack engineer who is availableon Instagram actively as @justmylittle_wonderwall_and you can read her @let_my_pen_talk

Neha Muthreja, from Nagpur.Currently, studying bachelor's of computer applications and has also completed her diploma in Mass communication. You can contact her on Instagram, User ID is muthreja_18.

Born Telanganite (Nizambadi).Daughter of KONKI JOHN SUBHAKER and ELIZABETH.

Loved to express her imagination through writing which was gifted by GOD.Completed her Masters in Eflu Lucknow. Her strength is younger SIBLING. She started writing from   2years back. Follow her on Your quote (Konki Kamal Sharon).

Shubham Shah, owner to @spicy_emotions , A 25 yr old guy who recently has entered,the digital platform of imprinting emotions. He says Writing has impersonated him since childhood And he has now been writing for over a decade! Cooking, on the other hand, is his passion! Share your reviews on his INSTAGRAM handle - @spicy_emotions Or via email on - shubham2shah@gmail.com

Bhavika SujitKumar Jain, student of BA.LL. From Nagpur loves to write because feels like it's a better way to express our love, emotion, Email.id: bhavikajain081@gmail.com

Swosti Trishna Mohanty, from Bhubaneswar, Odisha. Currently pursuing Bsc, Biotechnology.

Millie shukla(sarita), a passionate writer, a student persuing CA and CS. She is currently living in delhi and hometown is from lucknow. Her parents Shivdutt shukla and Sangeeta shukla are proud of her . She's an ambivert by nature and you can find her on instagram and yourquote.

Susmita Biswas writes short stories and poems. She is a graduate in computer engineering from West Bengal. Her mail id is: sbsusmi@gmail.com

Nikita Labhane from Ballarpur and she is persuading Nursing.

Suyashi Mishra, Lucknow, U.P. She is 22 years old, psychology major. Books allure her more than people. Mysteries of the universe and abandoned places captures her heart. Rivers, Oceans and lakes are her best friends. You can never know what's on her mind.

Vibah deshpande, A pharmacist by profession. I love reading books, music and love to write. I am a coffee lover, a rain gazer, a travel enthusiast and a keen observer of nature. I love to write little snippets of anything I find interesting. You can see some of my writings on my Instagram handle- 0@scribbledscriptsbyvd.

Shubahm kumar, a student. His passion is to write poetries, quotes and raps. And likes to cook and click good pictures around. He is interested in travelling the world as a YouTube blogger.

Nisha soni From bihar, siwan. She is studying in class 12th.

Sagar bhandare, A moody writer who is always in a mood of writing, writing is what keeps him alive.

Anmol pandey, Doctor by profession, writer by passion,

Kyuki jab ehsaas badhte h panne bharte Hain.

Vileshranjith, studying BCA 2nd year hailing from Bangalore is a person who is still working on accepting the real world around him but. He always has your back once he knows you are right for him. And always available for a random talk @mr_unpure_soul

Nikita Mukherjee of Pandaveswar, Pashchim Bardhaman. Is persuading her English Honours is in 3rd year.

Shatakshi, from Dilli (Delhi), currently trying to survive 11th grade. she writes and somedays, I want to make movies; apart totally obsessed with boy bands, Maggi and Oreos! You can contact her through email: shatakshi.vashishtha.dr@gmail.com

Subhodeep, Studied from R. K. Mission School. Now studying Marine Engineer from DMET. From Jamshedpur, Jharkhand.

Safiya Motiwala belongs to Surat, Gujarat. Has done her masters in commerce and is a teacher by profession.

The name is RK Nathan higher secondary dropout from 606001 with an Voter ID XAG0493585 using jio 638002476.A 90 Kid completed 27 years last feb,2019.

Astha Yadav is a content writer and she has participated in many anthologies as a co-author. And also compiled an anthology 'A beautiful mistake'. Earlier, writing was not a cup of tea for her but later she gained interest in diary writing and now she pour her heart out on her Instagram page @red_roses

Pranjal Bisht from Delhi belonging to city as beautiful as Uttrakhand. Studying in 11th standard as a Science student. Writing not for some specific reason but because she likes to and it makes her happy penning down the things that a going in and outside of her.

A 12 class medical student with ambitious soul. From Madhubani and lives in Delhi.

The journey from being Aditya to Arya Artis wasn't easy, the experience got poetry. Hip Hop added rap to it, Mother gave him wings to fly, Dad showed him the way to sky.

Prem Kumar and is a student , chess player and enthusiastic writer from Bokaro Steel City , Jharkhand . Well just , don't be a writer be a writing .

Being something different from others yet going through the same, DIPIKA GOUDA is here with all that, she need. Apsian, belongs to odisha and 12th class is her current qualification. Dancer and a writer by heart.

Riddhi Upadhyay, A designer by profession and A writer by heart. Lives in nawabo ka sheher Bhopal. And she is currently working with a gujrati designer.

Praharsha Isrupu, from Hyderabad she is a Civil aspirant.

Tasmayee Biswal, daughter of Tapan Biswal and Smita Mohanty, currently studying in class XI science at DAV public school, pokhariput, Bhubaneshwar. Writer by choice and without any regrets. Follow and like her quotes in https://www.yourquote.in/

Navrang Kailas Damodar from Nagpur , Maharashtra ,graduated in B.Sc., presently pursuing my master in Sociology, CSE aspirant.

Tanya Sen. A 14 aged student belonging to a small city Bhopal. Want to become become an artist that paints thoughts onto paper in form of words which are eternal.

Preeti, Born and brought up in Jamshedpur- the Steel City. Fled to Bhubaneshwar for persuing B.com. Currently in second year. Cooking conversations with future, daydreaming the impossible. Loves personifying things.. Obsessed with night sky. Bad habit since 2012..cannot skip writing diary everyday.

Ankur Sachan from Kanpur. A cricketer by lover and writer by heart. Words connect themselves with me. And also shoes are better than love they save you and never hurt you.

Shubham jain, currently compiling my book.

Sahil Sourav, a 1st-year law student exploring his interest in writing. He writes what he observes around himself. He fills the void in his life with caffeine and books. hope my story acts as a preclude to your world of imagination and helps you find yourself. You can contact him via Instagram- @sahilsourav7781

Hey!! This is Ishan nimdeokar he resides in Indore and is a student of Law, like to articulate things closely observed and inclined towards life. Email id: ishannimdeokar142@gmail.com

Nidhi Sugandh. Belongs to Nagpur the place which is famous for oranges.

She is pursuing BA 2nd year.

She is Deepshikha Agarwal from Bharuch Gujarat. A tutor who is preparing for bank exams. She has also got best student of the year and also first rank holder. She has completed my masters in accountancy and a writer and photographer by passion.. She is a happy go lucky and cheerful girl basically from Haryana, have lived in Assam and currently staying in Bharuch Gujarat since 17 yrs.

www.ingramcontent.com/pod-product-compliance
Lightning Source LLC
LaVergne TN
LVHW091606170726

843492LV00007B/2285